ROALD DAHL'S

FANTASTIC FAMILIES

working in partnership with
National Literacy Trust

ILLUSTRATED BY QUENTIN BLAKE

PUFFIN

PUFFIN BOOKS

UK | USA | Canada | Ireland | Australia
India | New Zealand | South Africa

Puffin Books is part of the Penguin Random House group of companies
whose addresses can be found at global.penguinrandomhouse.com.

puffinbooks.com

Made for McDonald's 2015
001

Charlie and the Chocolate Factory: first published in the USA by Alfred A. Knopf, Inc., 1964,
and in Great Britain by George Allen & Unwin 1967
Fantastic Mr Fox: first published in Great Britain by George Allen & Unwin 1970
Published in paperback by Puffin Books

Printed in Slovakia

A CIP catalogue record for this book is available from the British Library

ISBN: 978–0–141–36253–3

The National Literacy Trust is a registered charity no. 1116260 and a company limited
by guarantee no. 5836486 registered in England and Wales and a registered charity in
Scotland no. SC042944. Registered address: 68 South Lambeth Road, London SW8 1RL.
National Literacy Trust logo and reading tips copyright © National Literacy Trust, 2014

www.literacytrust.org.uk/donate

Batch nr.: 123913/16

Explore the extraordinary world of

ROALD DAHL

Meet two of the most
FANTASTIC FAMILIES ever.

Fantastic Mr Fox lives with **wonderful** Mrs Fox
and their four **resourceful** Small Foxes.
Are they **clever** and **cunning** enough to outwit
nasty farmers Boggis, Bunce and Bean who
have trapped the foxes in their hole?

Charlie Bucket doesn't have much,
but he **has** got **lovely** parents,
four **fantastic** grandparents and
a **big** imagination.

Bring Roald Dahl's extraordinary stories
to life with the **Happy Studio** app.
Simply download the app to a phone
or tablet and read the stories in this
book aloud to experience the fun.

Mr Fox and his Family

from

FANTASTIC MR FOX

On a hill above the valley there was
a wood.

In the wood there was a huge tree.

Under the tree there was a hole.

In the hole lived Mr Fox and
Mrs Fox and their four Small Foxes.

Every evening as soon as it got dark, Mr Fox would say to Mrs Fox, 'Well, my darling, what shall it be this time? A plump chicken from Boggis's farm? A duck or a goose from Bunce? Or a nice turkey from Bean?' And when Mrs Fox had told him what she wanted, Mr Fox would creep down

into the valley in the darkness of the night and help himself.

Boggis and Bunce and Bean knew very well what was going on, and it made them wild with rage. They were not men who liked to give anything away. Less still did they like anything to be stolen from them. So every night each of them would take his shotgun and hide in a dark place somewhere on his own farm, hoping to catch the robber.

But Mr Fox was too clever for them. He always approached a farm with

the wind blowing in his face, and this
meant that if any man were lurking in
the shadows ahead, the wind would
carry the smell of that man to Mr Fox's
nose from far away. Thus, if Mr Boggis
was hiding behind his Chicken House
Number One, Mr Fox would smell him

out from fifty yards off and quickly change direction, heading for Chicken House Number Four at the other end of the farm.

'Dang and blast that lousy beast!' cried Boggis.

'I'd like to rip his guts out!' said Bunce.

'He must be killed!' cried Bean.

'But how?' said Boggis. 'How on earth can we catch the blighter?'

Bean picked his nose delicately with a long finger. 'I have a plan,' he said.

'You've never had a decent plan yet,' said Bunce.

'Shut up and listen,' said Bean. 'Tomorrow night we will all hide just outside the hole where the fox lives. We will wait there until he comes out. Then . . . *Bang! Bang-bang-bang.*'

The farmers' waiting-game went on for three days and three nights.

Down in the hole, Mr Fox had not spoken for a long time. He had been sitting quite still, his eyes closed, not even hearing what the others were saying. Mrs Fox knew that he was trying desperately to think of a way out. And now, as she looked at him, she saw him stir himself and get slowly to his feet. He looked back at his wife. There was a little spark of excitement dancing in his eyes.

'What is it, darling?' said Mrs Fox quickly.

'I've just had a bit of an idea,' Mr Fox said carefully.

'What?' cried the Small Foxes. 'Oh, Dad, what is it?'

'Come *on*!' said Mrs Fox. 'Tell us quickly!'

'Well . . .' said Mr Fox, then he stopped and sighed and sadly shook his head. He sat down again. 'It's no good,' he said. 'It won't work after all.'

'Why not, Dad?'

'Because it means so much digging and we aren't any of us strong enough for that after three days and nights without food.'

'Yes we are, Dad!' cried the Small Foxes, jumping up and running to their father. 'We can do it! You see if we can't! So can you!'

Mr Fox looked at the four Small Foxes and he smiled. 'What fine children I have,' he thought. 'They are starving to death and they haven't had a drink for three days, but they are still undefeated. I must not let them down.'

'I . . . I suppose we could give it a try,' he said.

'Let's go, Dad! Tell us what you

want us to do!'

Slowly, Mrs Fox got to her feet. She was suffering more than any of them from the lack of food and water. She was very weak. 'I am so sorry,' she said, 'but I don't think I am going to be much help.'

'You stay right where you are, my darling,' said Mr Fox. 'We can handle this by ourselves.

'We must go in a very special direction,'

said Mr Fox, pointing sideways and downward.

'Dad, I wish you would tell us *where* we are going,' said one of the children.

'I dare not do that,' said Mr Fox, 'because this place I am *hoping* to get to is so *marvellous* that if I described it to you now you would go crazy with excitement. And then, if we failed to get there (which is very possible), you would die of disappointment. I don't want to raise your hopes too much, my darlings.'

For a long, long time they kept on digging. For how long they did not know, because there were no days and no nights down there in the murky tunnel. But at last Mr Fox gave the order to stop.

Can we please have **colourful** coats?

'I think,' he said, 'we had better take a peep upstairs now and see where we are. I know where I *want* to be, but I can't possibly be sure we're anywhere near it.'

Slowly, wearily, the foxes began to slope the tunnel up towards the surface. Up and up it went . . . until suddenly they came to something hard above their heads and they couldn't go up any further. Mr Fox reached up to examine this hard thing. 'It's wood!' he whispered. 'Wooden planks!'

'What does that mean, Dad?'

'It means, unless I am very much mistaken, that we are right underneath somebody's house,' whispered Mr Fox. 'Be very quiet now while I take a peek.'

Carefully, Mr Fox began pushing up one of the floorboards. The board

creaked most terribly and they all ducked down, waiting for something awful to happen. Nothing did. So Mr Fox pushed up a second board. And then, very, very cautiously, he poked his head up through the gap. He let out a shriek of excitement.

'*I've done it!*' he yelled. 'I've done it *first time*! *I've done it! I've done it!*' He pulled himself up through the gap in the floor and started prancing and dancing with joy. 'Come on up!' he sang out. 'Come up and see where

you are, my darlings! What a sight for a hungry fox! Hallelujah! Hooray! Hooray!'

The four Small Foxes scrambled up out of the tunnel and what a fantastic sight it was that now met their eyes! They were in a huge shed and the whole place was teeming with chickens. There were white chickens and brown chickens and black chickens by the thousand!

'Boggis's Chicken House Number One!' cried Mr Fox. 'It's exactly what

I was aiming at! I hit it slap in the
middle! First time! Isn't that fantastic!
And, if I may say so, rather clever!'

The **Fox family** have to make a
dramatic escape from the farmers.

Do you have the
Happy Studio app
downloaded?
Launch it **now** for
an **extra** activity!

Can you imagine your own **fantastic** family having an **extraordinary** adventure together and draw it here?

Meet the Buckets

from

CHARLIE AND THE
CHOCOLATE FACTORY

These two
very old
people
are the
father and mother of Mr Bucket.
Their names are Grandpa Joe and
Grandma Josephine.

And *these* two very old people are
the father and mother of Mrs Bucket.
Their names are
Grandpa George
and Grandma
Georgina.

This is Mr Bucket.
This is Mrs Bucket.
Mr and Mrs
Bucket have
a small boy
whose name
is Charlie Bucket.
This is Charlie.
How d'you do? And
how d'you do? And
how d'you do again?
He is pleased to
meet you.

The whole of this family – the six grown-ups and little Charlie Bucket – live together in a small wooden house on the edge of a great town.

The house wasn't nearly large enough for so many people, and life was extremely uncomfortable for them all. There were only two rooms in the place altogether, and there was only one bed. The bed was given to the four old grandparents because they were so old and tired. They were so tired, they never got out of it.

Grandpa Joe and Grandma Josephine on one side, Grandpa George and Grandma Georgina on the other side.

Mr and Mrs Bucket and little Charlie Bucket slept in the other room, upon mattresses on the floor.

In the summertime, this wasn't too bad, but in the winter, freezing cold draughts blew across the floor all night long, and it was awful.

There wasn't any question of them being able to buy a better house – or even one more bed to sleep in. They were far too poor for that.

Mr Bucket was the only person in the family with a job. He worked in a toothpaste factory, where he sat all day long at a bench and screwed the little caps on to the tops of the tubes of toothpaste after the tubes had been filled.

But a toothpaste cap-screwer is never paid very much money, and poor Mr Bucket, however hard he worked, and however fast he screwed on the caps, was never able to make enough to buy one half of the things that so large a family needed. There wasn't even enough money to buy proper food for them all. The only meals they could afford were bread and margarine for breakfast, boiled potatoes and cabbage for lunch, and cabbage soup for supper. Sundays were a bit better.

They all looked forward to Sundays because then, although they had exactly the same, everyone was allowed a second helping.

The Buckets, of course, didn't starve, but every one of them – the two old grandfathers, the two old grandmothers, Charlie's father, Charlie's mother, and especially little Charlie

himself – went about from morning till night with a horrible empty feeling in their tummies.

Charlie felt it worst of all. And although his father and mother often went without their own share of lunch or supper so that they could give it to him, it still wasn't nearly enough for a growing boy. He desperately wanted something more filling and satisfying than cabbage and cabbage soup. The one thing he longed for more than anything else was . . . CHOCOLATE.

Walking to school in the mornings, Charlie could see great slabs of chocolate piled up high in the shop windows, and he would stop and stare and press his nose against the glass, his mouth watering like mad.

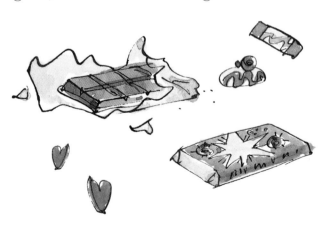

Many times a day, he would see other children taking bars of creamy chocolate out of their pockets and munching them greedily, and *that*, of course, was *pure* torture.

Only once a year, on his birthday, did Charlie Bucket ever get to taste a bit of chocolate. The whole family saved up their money for that special occasion, and when the great day arrived, Charlie was always presented with one small chocolate bar to eat all by himself. And each time he received it, on those marvellous birthday mornings, he would place it carefully in a small wooden box that he owned, and treasure it as though it were a bar of solid gold; and for the next few days, he would allow himself only to look at it, but never to touch it. Then at last, when he could stand it no longer, he would peel back a *tiny* bit of the paper wrapping at

41

one corner to expose a *tiny* bit of chocolate, and then he would take a *tiny* nibble – just enough to allow the lovely sweet taste to spread out slowly over his tongue. The next day, he would take another tiny nibble, and so on, and so on. And in this way, Charlie would make his sixpenny bar of birthday chocolate last him for more than a month.

But I haven't yet told you about the one awful thing that tortured little Charlie, the lover of chocolate, more than *anything* else. This thing, for him, was far, far worse than seeing slabs of chocolate in the shop windows or watching other children munching bars of creamy chocolate right in front of him. It was the most terrible torturing thing you could imagine, and it was this:

In the town itself, actually within *sight* of the house in which Charlie lived, there was an ENORMOUS CHOCOLATE FACTORY!

Just imagine that!

And it wasn't simply an ordinary enormous chocolate factory, either. It was the largest and most famous in the whole world! It was WONKA'S FACTORY, owned by a man called Mr Willy Wonka, the greatest inventor and maker of chocolates that there has ever been. And what a tremendous, marvellous place it was! It had huge iron gates leading into it, and a high

wall surrounding it, and smoke
belching from its chimneys, and
strange whizzing sounds coming from
deep inside it. And outside the walls,
for half a mile
around in every
direction, the
air was
scented with
the heavy
rich smell of
melting
chocolate!

Twice a day, on his way to and from school, little Charlie Bucket had to walk right past the gates of the factory. And every time he went by, he would begin to walk very, very slowly, and he would hold his nose high in the air and take long deep sniffs of the gorgeous chocolatey smell all around him.

Oh, how he loved that smell!

And oh, how he wished he could go inside the factory and see what it was like!

In the evenings, after he had finished his supper of watery cabbage soup, Charlie always went into the room of his four grandparents to listen to their stories, and then afterwards to say good night.

One evening, when Charlie went in to see his grandparents, he said to them, 'Is it *really* true that Wonka's

Chocolate Factory is the biggest in the world?'

'*True?*' cried all four of them at once. 'Of course it's true! Good heavens, didn't you know *that*? It's about *fifty* times as big as any other!'

'And is Mr Willy Wonka *really* the cleverest chocolate maker in the world?'

'My *dear* boy,' said Grandpa Joe, raising himself up a little higher on his pillow, 'Mr Willy Wonka is the most *amazing*, the most *fantastic*, the most *extraordinary* chocolate maker the world has ever seen! I thought *everybody* knew that!'

'I knew he was famous, Grandpa Joe, and I knew he was very clever . . .'

'*Clever!*' cried the old man. 'He's more than that! He's a *magician* with chocolate! He can make *anything* – anything he wants! Isn't that a fact, my dears?'

The other three old people nodded their heads slowly up and down, and said, '*Absolutely* true. *Just* as true as can be.'

And Grandpa Joe said, 'You mean to say I've never *told* you about Mr Willy Wonka and his factory?'

'Never,' answered little Charlie.

'Good heavens above! I don't know what's the matter with me!'

'Will you tell me now, Grandpa Joe, please?'

'I certainly will. Sit down beside me on the bed, my dear, and listen carefully.'

Grandpa Joe was the oldest of the four grandparents. He was ninety-six and a half, and that is just about as old as anybody can be. Like all extremely old people, he was delicate and weak, and throughout the day he spoke very little. But in the evenings, when Charlie, his beloved grandson, was in the room, he seemed in some marvellous way to

grow quite young again. All his tiredness fell away from him, and he became as eager and excited as a young boy.

'Oh, what a man he is, this Mr Willy Wonka!' cried Grandpa Joe. 'Did you know, for example, that he has himself invented more than two hundred new kinds of chocolate bars, each with a different centre, each far sweeter and creamier and more delicious than anything the other chocolate factories can make!'

'Perfectly true!' cried Grandma Josephine. 'And he sends them to *all* the four corners of the earth! Isn't that so, Grandpa Joe?'

'It is, my dear, it is. And to all the kings and presidents of the world as well. But it isn't only chocolate bars that he makes. Oh, dear me, no! He

has some really *fantastic* inventions up his sleeve, Mr Willy Wonka has! Did you know that he's invented a way of making chocolate ice cream so that it stays cold for hours and hours without being in the refrigerator? You can even leave it lying in the sun all morning on a hot day and it won't go runny!'

'But that's *impossible*!' said little Charlie, staring at his grandfather.

'Of course it's impossible!' cried Grandpa Joe. 'It's completely *absurd*!

But Mr Willy Wonka has done it!'

'Quite right!' the others agreed, nodding their heads. 'Mr Wonka has done it.'

'And then again,' Grandpa Joe went on, speaking very slowly now so that Charlie wouldn't miss a word, 'Mr Willy Wonka can make marshmallows that taste of violets, and rich caramels that change colour every ten seconds as you suck them, and little feathery sweets that melt away deliciously the moment you put them between your lips. He can make chewing-gum that never loses its taste, and sugar balloons that you can blow up to enormous sizes before you pop them with a pin and gobble them up. And, by a most secret method, he can make lovely blue birds' eggs with black spots on them, and when you put one of these in your mouth, it gradually gets smaller and smaller until suddenly there is nothing left except a tiny little pink sugary baby bird sitting on the tip of your tongue.'

Grandpa Joe paused and ran the point of his tongue slowly over his lips. 'It makes my mouth water just *thinking* about it,' he said.

'Mine, too,' said little Charlie.

Just then, Mr Bucket, Charlie's father, came into the room. He was home from the toothpaste factory, and he was waving an evening newspaper rather excitedly. 'Have you heard the news?' he cried. He held up the paper so that they could see the huge headline.

WONKA FACTORY TO BE OPENED
AT LAST TO LUCKY FEW

'You mean people are actually going
to be allowed to go inside the factory?'
cried Grandpa Joe. 'Read us what it
says – quickly!'

'All right,' said Mr Bucket. 'Listen.'

*Mr Willy Wonka, the confectionery genius
whom nobody has seen for the last ten years,
sent out the following notice today:*

Evening Bulletin

I, Willy Wonka, have decided to allow five children – just five, mind you, and no more – to visit my factory this year. These lucky five will be shown around personally by me, and they will be allowed to see all the secrets and the magic of my factory. Then, at the end of the tour, as a special present, all of them will be given enough chocolates and sweets to last them for the rest of their lives! So watch out for the Golden Tickets! Five Golden Tickets have been printed on golden paper, and these five Golden Tickets have been hidden underneath the ordinary wrapping paper of five ordinary bars of chocolate. These five chocolate bars may be anywhere – in any shop in any street in any town in any country in the world – upon any counter where Wonka's Sweets are sold. And the five lucky finders of these five Golden Tickets are the only ones who will be allowed to visit my factory and see what it's like now inside! Good luck to you all, and happy hunting! (Signed Willy Wonka.)

If you won a **Golden Ticket** that would allow you and your family to visit any **extraordinary** place in the world, where would you like to go and why?

....

....

....

....

....

....

....

....

Do you have the **Happy Studio** app downloaded? Launch it **now** for an **extra** activity!

Have some more fun with these
FANTASTIC FAMILIES!

The **Happy Studio** app has extra
activities linked to this book.
Download it now to
a phone or tablet.

And you can delve deeper
into the extraordinary world of

ROALD DAHL

at www.roalddahl.com